Follow Me

Sheila O'Flanagan lives in Dublin. She is a number one bestselling author and writes about families, relationships and finding love. She worked in finance before becoming a full-time writer and has sold over four million copies of her books.

Follow Me

Sheila O'Flanagan

headline
review

First published in 2011
by HEADLINE REVIEW
An imprint of HEADLINE PUBLISHING GROUP

1

ISBN 978 0 7553 5931 8

Typeset by Palimpsest Book Production Limited, Falkirk, Stirlingshire
Printed and bound in Great Britain by Clays Ltd, St Ives plc

Headline's policy is to use papers that are natural, renewable and
recyclable products and made from wood grown in sustainable
forests. The logging and manufacturing processes are expected to
conform to the environmental regulations of the country of origin.

HEADLINE PUBLISHING GROUP
An Hachette UK Company
338 Euston Road
London NW1 3BH

www.headline.co.uk
www.hachette.co.uk

Follow Me

Chapter One

Pippa Jones was sitting in the bar of the Hyatt hotel in Birmingham. She was sipping a cup of tea and flicking through a tabloid newspaper that someone had left behind. Pippa knew that she should have been reading her work report, but the headline on the front page of the paper was too much to resist. It said 'Problems Playing Away' and it was about a well-known Premiership footballer who was having an affair.

Pippa wondered why it was that people with such glitzy lives always seemed to mess them up. Why did rich, handsome men who were married to stunning women need to have affairs? Why did they spend so much time in nightclubs with their mates? Why didn't they go home to their gorgeous wives?

If he was my husband, Pippa thought, I'd kill him for being in a nightclub without me. Then she laughed at herself, because the chances of her having a husband, no matter where he spent his time, were pretty remote. She didn't even have a boyfriend right now, and there seemed no chance of finding one either. She was far too busy these days to bother with boyfriends.

Pippa folded the paper and glanced at her watch. It was nearly seven o'clock and she was starting to feel hungry. She didn't want to eat in the hotel, so she left the newspaper on the table, then picked up her bag and walked outside. It had been a warm midsummer day and the evening air was still very pleasant. She made her way along Broad Street, then crossed the road and strolled by the canal. There were lots of people sitting at the tables outside the pubs and restaurants that lined the banks. It might be difficult, thought Pippa, to find somewhere free, but then two people got up from a table. She slid into one of the empty seats before anyone else could take it.

She sat back and stretched her bare legs out in front of her. They had a light, natural tan. Her left leg also had a bruise high up, from where she'd walked into a desk at the office. She had a terrible habit of doing that. Richard, her boss, said it was because she was always in a hurry and didn't look where she was going. Pippa smiled to herself. He might be right, but she wasn't in a hurry now. She'd finished her work for the day and could relax at last.

She looked up from her legs and spotted her reflection in the window opposite. The glass made her look a bit fatter and shorter than she really was, so she sat up straighter. It didn't make as much difference as she'd hoped. She could see a woman who looked somewhere between twenty-five and thirty-five, with curly red hair. The woman was wearing a plain white T-shirt, short denim skirt and blue flip-flops.

Her reflection was more or less right. Pippa Jones was twenty-nine years old. She'd changed into the T-shirt, skirt and flip-flops when she'd returned to the hotel a couple of hours earlier. Until then she'd been wearing a navy suit, white blouse and high-heeled navy shoes from Office. Her working uniform, she liked to call it. She was staying at the Hyatt hotel because she'd been meeting customers in Birmingham all day.

Pippa Jones was a sales rep. More than just a rep. Her actual title was Senior Sales Consultant, and she was very good at her job. Last year she had been the person with the highest sales figures in her company. As a result, she'd won an all-expenses-paid trip to Paris for the weekend. She planned to be the best sales-person this year too. The company was offering a week in New York to anyone who beat Pippa's record sales of the year before. She wanted to

3

beat them herself. She was very competitive, and she'd always wanted to go to New York.

Pippa's company sold computer security systems. Pippa liked both sales and messing about with computers, which meant she also liked her job. She would go into a would-be customer's office, look at their system and then hack into it, even if they already had software security in place. They were usually horrified. Then she would tell them about Defender, her company's product, and offer it to them on a trial basis. Ninety per cent of the customers bought it afterwards, which was why Pippa was so successful.

Pippa's job took her all around the country. Last week she'd been in Dover, seeing her very best customer; the week before in Bristol and today in Birmingham. It was just as well, she thought, that she enjoyed driving.

A waiter came over and she ordered a burger with salad and a glass of sparkling water. She really would have preferred chips with her burger, but the sight of her reflection had put her off chips. Besides, salad was nice on a sunny day, and choosing it instead of chips made her feel good.

She watched the passers-by as she waited for her food to arrive. There were lots of couples, strolling hand in hand alongside the canal. They were laughing and joking with each other as they followed the waterway. Sometimes they even stopped and kissed each other. You wouldn't think, Pippa thought, that you were in the middle of a big city here. The sun sparkling off the water and the passing chug of a barge made you feel as though you were in the country. She felt lucky that she had a job that allowed her to enjoy moments like this.

The waiter returned with the water which she sipped slowly as she carried on watching the people around her. It was lovely to be outdoors, she thought. Eating outside somehow made her feel even more as if she was in the country.

Pippa wasn't a country girl, although some of her London friends told her that she was. She'd been brought up in Bexley, which was only seventeen miles outside the capital. Her mum insisted that it had pretty much been in the country when they'd first moved there. Her mum had moved to England from Galway, in Ireland. Her dad was from Cardiff. They told her that she had Celtic blood in her. That explained why her hair was red and why she was as good as the boys in a fight.

Pippa didn't think that being good in a fight was anything to do with Celtic blood. She thought it was because she was the only girl among five brothers. She'd had to be a bit tough to make her voice heard.

The house where she'd grown up was a neat semi on a small estate. It backed on to a large field. The field had once been part of a farm, but for as long as Pippa could remember it had been owned by a horse-riding school. She'd gone to the school when she'd been younger. She'd enjoyed riding horses and looking at them from her back bedroom window.

These days, the view from her bedroom window was different. She lived in a one-bedroomed flat in Shepherd's Bush. All she could see from her window was the house that backed on to it, but she didn't mind. She liked the city. She liked living on her own. She thought that might be because it had been hard to find time to be alone when she was growing up at home.

In Bexley, there had always been someone rushing in and out of the house. Always someone shouting about something. There had never been any real privacy. Sometimes she missed the noise and the bustle, but not very often. She tried to go home to her parents' house once a month, because she liked her mum fussing over her. (Also, Betty Jones was much better at washing and ironing than Pippa. Whenever she left Bexley, all her white blouses were crisply laundered.) Three of her brothers still lived at home too, which meant there was still plenty of noise. So it was fun for a weekend, but nice to come back to the peace and quiet of her flat too.

Being by herself allowed Pippa to do whatever she liked. It allowed her to spend lots of time doing things she enjoyed, like surfing the net or reading the latest bestseller without having to worry about anyone else. It allowed her to spend lots of time at her job. Of course, it wasn't all work when she was in London. She had friends in the city. None of them were from her office. Pam, Jane, Lissa and Sherry all had different jobs. The girls liked getting together to talk about work and boyfriends and holidays and clothes. Pippa enjoyed meeting them, even if they did sometimes give her a hard time. They teased her because she spent more time worrying about her sales figures than her own figure, and because she hadn't even gone out for a drink with a man for over a year.

'I don't have time,' she told Lissa sternly one evening. They'd gone to All Bar One and she'd had more wine than she had intended. 'I have a career.'

'Hey, we all have careers!' Lissa worked for the local council. 'None of us have time, but it's important to have someone.'

Pippa wasn't so sure. Her last relationship, with a guy called Mark, had broken up messily when she found out he was two-timing her. That was the thing about men, she thought. Even men who weren't rich footballers with temptation in their way. They all seemed to be programmed to cheat on you, and then say it wasn't their fault! Mark had blamed her for the break-up. He'd said that she'd driven him into another woman's arms. That she was too bossy and too competitive, and that she was away too much. She knew he was right about some of it, but she was annoyed that he thought it was a good reason to cheat on her.

She hadn't bothered with anyone after Mark. He'd been the last in the line of men Pippa had gone out with but who weren't ever going to be really special. All of them had complained about her job. They didn't like her being on the road. So she'd decided to work harder. If work was the cause of men breaking up with her, then she had to make it worth it.

That was when Pippa's sales numbers had started to go higher and higher, which had ended up in her winning the trip to Paris. Sherry had come with her because she didn't have a boyfriend to bring. It served Mark right, Pippa thought, that he wasn't with her in the world's most romantic city. She didn't care that she was there with her friend instead. They'd had a great time seeing the sights and drooling over the sexy French men.

When she came back from Paris, she decided that she'd do even better with her sales the next year. When she heard about the New York prize, she was thrilled but it wasn't all about the trips. Pippa really did like hacking into computers, and she liked selling security software. She knew that Sherry and the others thought she was a bit weird for enjoying something that seemed so boring. Sometimes they called her a geek or a nerd, but she didn't care.

Her burger arrived. It looked a bit lonely on the plate with just a bit of salad beside it. Pippa couldn't see her reflection any more, so she asked the waiter if she could have some chips on the side. After all, she thought, I've had a busy day. I deserve some comfort food.

She picked at the salad and watched people walking along the banks of the canal while she waited for the chips. She smiled when the waiter brought them. They were big and fat, the sort

9

of chips she liked best. He asked her if she'd like something to read as she was on her own. She nodded and he brought her a gossip magazine.

Pippa didn't normally bother with gossip magazines. She didn't really care about celebrities, but, like with the tabloid newspaper earlier, it was hard to stop reading when you started. The glossy magazine's main story was about an *X Factor* winner and her new diet. Pippa couldn't see why the pretty girl needed to be on a diet at all. In fact, she thought, if I had a figure like hers, I'd be very happy. But to have a figure like hers I'd probably have to stop eating chips, which would be a shame!

She finished the burger and chips and asked for the bill. She paid by credit card and then stood up.

'Are you leaving?'

A tall, fair-haired man, who'd stopped near the table, asked the question. He was wearing cargo pants, a faded blue T-shirt and an old pair of trainers. His eyes matched the blue of his top. Pippa wondered if he knew how good-looking he was. Probably, she thought. Men always thought they looked great, even when they didn't, but he definitely did.

'Are you?' he asked again.

She nodded.

'Do you mind if I nab this table? They're in short supply.'

'Of course not,' she said. 'Everyone wants to eat outside on such a nice day.'

'Great.' He sat down in the seat she'd just got up from. 'Thanks.'

'You're welcome.'

Pippa began to walk away.

'Excuse me!' he called after her.

She turned around again. For a split second she imagined him asking her to join him for a drink, but that was a silly thought, and of course he didn't.

'You've left this behind.' He held up the glossy magazine.

'It's not mine,' she told him. 'It belongs to the restaurant.'

'Oh, good. Something to read.'

She smiled to herself. She didn't think he'd be very interested in the magazine's stories about clothes and diets. It was funny how different men and women were about things like that. She wasn't into clothes or diets herself, but she loved reading about other people's. She turned away again and headed back towards the hotel. It had been a busy day and Pippa had a long drive ahead of her in the morning.

She was going to go back to her room, watch some TV and get an early night. She was going to stop thinking about the handsome stranger sitting at the table beside the canal.

Chapter Two

Pippa saw the good-looking man again the next morning. She'd just finished paying her hotel bill and was leaving the reception desk when he arrived there too. At first she didn't recognise him, because he was wearing a dark suit, a white shirt and a red tie. His hair, which had been loose and floppy the evening before, was carefully gelled. His shoes were shiny and he was carrying a black leather briefcase.

Pippa was surprised. Even though she'd barely spoken to him the evening before, she'd got the impression that he was a relaxed, laid-back sort of person. He didn't seem like a shiny-shoes, briefcase-carrying type of guy. She supposed she'd probably looked relaxed and laid back yesterday too, in her short skirt and flip-flops.

Today, like him, Pippa was wearing a suit, although she wasn't carrying a briefcase. Her curly red hair was pulled neatly into a bun on the back of her head. So even if the man noticed her, he probably wouldn't have recognised her either. Not that she especially wanted him to recognise her or anything! It was just that the chance seeing of him at her hotel surprised her.

Pippa put the blue-eyed stranger out of her head as she got into her car. She enjoyed driving and didn't mind the journey back to London. It wasn't a direct drive back because she was calling in to see potential clients on the way. She had meetings arranged in Milton Keynes and in Luton. She knew that it would be late by the time she eventually made it back to her Shepherd's Bush flat, but that was OK. She was looking forward to the day ahead.

It was glorious weather again. The air was warm and the sun shone from a china-blue sky. Pippa put on her sunglasses to protect her eyes from the glare. She punched her destinations into her sat nav and eased into the heavy traffic leaving Birmingham.

She didn't relax until she'd reached the motorway. Then she switched the car stereo on and began listening to her *Best of Crystal Gayle* CD.

She sang along happily, even though she knew she had a terrible voice. Pippa had been thrown out of the school choir because she couldn't keep in tune, but singing on her own was different. There was nobody to upset with her bum notes, and she liked belting out 'Don't It Make My Brown Eyes Blue'. It had been the song that had got her through her break-up with Mark. She gritted her teeth as she thought of him. He hadn't crossed her mind in ages.

The CD, on shuffle, changed track. Pippa overtook a lorry then moved back to the inside lane. She wasn't in that much of a hurry. She just hated being stuck behind lorries.

The CD had ended by the time Pippa turned towards the business park where her first potential customer had its offices. She parked in the car park and hurried into the modern building. The company was a small one but kept all of its records on computer.

'We're very eco-friendly,' the young Managing Director explained. 'We don't print out anything unless it's really necessary.'

'That's why you need to be very careful with your digital files,' Pippa told him cheerfully as she hacked into his laptop and opened a file marked 'Confidential'.

By the time she left Milton Keynes, she was certain that she would close a deal with the eco-friendly company. There was also the possibility of two more contracts with other firms she'd visited. The key to being a successful sales rep, Pippa told herself, was knowing your customers and their needs.

Luton was Pippa's next stop. This time the business park was on the outskirts of the town, which meant that it overlooked green fields. There were fountains and plazas between the buildings too, and Pippa thought it would be a nice place to work. She pulled into a parking bay outside one of the low-rise office blocks, then checked her BlackBerry mobile phone to make sure she had the right contact information. She got out of her car and locked the door.

She gave her name to the girl at the reception desk, who wrote it on a badge and told her to take a seat for a moment. Pippa pinned the badge to her jacket and sat down to wait in one of the leather chairs.

'Don't It Make My Brown Eyes Blue' was still going round in Pippa's head. She tapped her fingers gently on her smart skirt and hummed beneath her breath.

A door opened and she glanced up. Then she stared. The dishy man from her hotel in Birmingham had just walked out. She recognised him straightaway. He was shaking hands with a woman and telling her he'd be in touch. He said something that Pippa couldn't hear, and the woman smiled at him and then laughed. From the look on the woman's face, Pippa could see that she was attracted to him. Hard not to be, she admitted to herself. He was very handsome!

She watched him as he strode across the reception area. He was looking straight ahead of him and hadn't seen her. He pushed open the glass door and stepped outside. Pippa could still see him as he unlocked a red car and got into the driver's seat.

That's so weird, she thought, seeing him again. Spooky even.

'Miss Jones?' The receptionist called her. 'Mrs Bond will see you now.'

Tessa Bond was the IT Manager for the company. She was the blonde woman Pippa had seen talking to the mystery man. Pippa wanted to ask Tessa about him but she didn't. She told herself to keep her mind on her job. Unknown men weren't part of it, and they weren't important. So she put the guy out of her head.

She successfully hacked into Tessa Bond's computer and told her that Defender would protect her files. She also told her that her password, Bond 007, wasn't really that clever. She personally knew two other people who used it.

'It's easy to remember,' protested Tessa.

'And easy to guess,' said Pippa.

Tessa nodded. 'I suppose so.'

'Defender comes with a special electronic card that creates a new password for you every time you sign on to the secure area of your computer,' Pippa told her.

'What if I lose the card?' asked Tessa.

'You can apply for a new one online and it will be with you the next day,' said Pippa.

'It's not a cheap service.' Tessa was looking at the leaflet in front of her.

'It's the best,' Pippa told her.

'I don't know if we need something so complex.'

'How much would it cost your firm if all your information was stolen?' asked Pippa.

Tessa sighed. 'You have a point.'

'I know,' said Pippa.

'I'll call you,' promised Tessa. 'I need to talk to our accountant. He's a bit of a dragon.'

'I can talk to him with you, if you like,' Pippa said.

Tessa frowned. Then she picked up the phone.

A few minutes later, a middle-aged man walked into the office. He looked exactly how Pippa thought an accountant should look. He wore a white shirt and a blue tie. He pushed his gold-rimmed glasses up on his nose as Tessa explained about the computer security system.

'I thought we were looking at a different one,' he said. 'A cheaper one.'

'We were,' said Tessa. 'Safety Net, but ...'

'... ours is the best,' said Pippa firmly, 'and worth every penny.'

The accountant looked doubtful. He made some sharp comments about the cost, but an hour later, Pippa was leaving the business park with a smile on her face. The company had decided to buy her system after all. Tessa Bond had been very impressed with it, and in the end, the accountant had agreed that it was by far the most secure. Pippa had pointed out all the extra features that Defender had over Safety Net. She made him realise they were worth the extra money.

The meeting in Luton was her last of the day. She changed the CD to Emmylou Harris and sang along to 'Love Hurts' as she drove to Defender's offices near Latimer Road. She went inside. Her boss Richard was still at his desk. She gave him the good news about the signed contract. Then she told him about her meetings in Birmingham. She expected that at least two other companies would use their security software. They were big companies and couldn't make a decision on the spot like the one in Luton. The contracts would be worth a lot if they signed up.

'Another good week's work,' said Richard. He sounded pleased. 'So go home now and put your feet up, Pippa. Have a relaxing weekend.'

She nodded. 'That's exactly what I have planned.'

'Well done,' said Richard.

'Thanks.'

She walked out of the office and on to the street. She always left her car in the car park at work because it wasn't worth bringing it back to her flat. Parking was too difficult on her road and it was only a ten-minute walk away. Besides, it was nice to walk when she'd been driving all day, especially as it was still sunny and warm.

Her flat was the ground-floor level of a red-brick building. The best thing about it was that she had access to a long strip of garden. Even though she didn't know much about gardening, she liked having the outside space. She opened the door and walked outside. A black and white cat was stretched out in the shade of a rose bush. Pippa shared ownership of the cat with Anita, who lived in the upstairs flat. The cat shared his affection between both of them. He'd arrived as a wet, shivering stray one winter's evening. They'd both heard the mewing outside and had taken him in and fed him. They'd called him Hobo and allowed him to spend the night in the house. After he'd gone out the next day they hadn't expected him to return. However, he took up residence in the garden and didn't mind which of the girls fed him.

It was a good arrangement for everyone. Anita was an actress. Like Pippa she was often away, but one of them was nearly always around to feed Hobo and tickle him under his chin.

'I had a good day today,' Pippa told him as he opened his eyes to look at her. 'Lots of new business.'

Hobo yawned and started to wash his face. Pippa sometimes felt that the cat was critical of her life. That, like her ex-boyfriends, he didn't like her being away so much. He hadn't been fond of Mark, though. He'd mewed angrily whenever he was around. When they'd split up, Hobo had spent a lot of time sitting on her lap, comforting her. For a long time she'd allowed him to do that while she'd sat and stared into space. Lately she'd shooed him off her lap so that she could read through her business reports.

'It's not my fault,' she said. 'I'm trying to win a holiday to New York.'

Then she thought that maybe Hobo didn't want her to win a holiday to New York. 'I deserve it,' she told the cat sternly.

She went back into the flat and changed into jeans and a top before picking up a block of drawing paper and some pencils and going into the garden again. Pippa sat down opposite Hobo and began to draw him. Her pencil was quick over the paper and soon she had a perfect sketch of the sleeping cat. She had always been good at drawing, and she enjoyed sketching Hobo.

She smiled at her sketch, then turned over the page and started drawing again. This time the finished picture was of the man she'd seen in Birmingham and in the offices of her customers earlier. The face that looked back at her from the page was very attractive. She looked at it for a moment, then tore it off and rolled it into a ball. She threw it towards Hobo, who swatted it away. She was being silly about this man, Pippa told herself. Just because he was good-looking. Just because she'd liked the way he smiled. She sighed, and reminded herself that she was never going to be silly about a man again. She had far more important things in her life to worry about than them.

Chapter Three

Since her break-up with Mark, Pippa sometimes felt lonely at the weekends. She liked
spending time on Facebook and other
networking sites, but she also liked talking to
real people. There were some weekends when
she didn't talk to anyone at all. The weekends she didn't go home, or the weekends
that the girls all had dates. There were times
when she was happy with this. Other times
she wondered if she was the only girl in the
world watching TV by herself on a Saturday
night. Those times she thought she was a total
loser.

However, this weekend she didn't feel like a
loser and she didn't mind whether she was on
her own or not.

She spent Saturday morning cleaning her flat,
which she had neglected over the past few
weeks because she was travelling so much. She
quite enjoyed cleaning and tidying, because she
liked things around her to be neat. Sometimes
her friends teased her for being so tidy. They

called her a neat geek, but Pippa would point out that she lived in a small space and everything needed to have its own place. Anyway, she'd always been a tidy person. Even when she was younger, her mother never had to yell at her to clean up her room.

After she'd finished her clean-up she went clothes shopping. She wasn't as good at buying as she was at selling. She was never quite sure whether the clothes she tried on really suited her. That was why she wore navy suits all the time at work and jeans or denim skirts at home. She was confident about the suits and the jeans and the denim skirts. However, with the nicer weather, Pippa wanted some lighter clothes. So she spent the afternoon wandering around the shops, looking at shorts and flimsy skirts. In the end she decided her bum was too big for the micro shorts that seemed to be in fashion right now. She bought two colourful summer skirts in Topshop, as well as some light tops to go with them. She hoped that the nice weather would continue. It was funny, she thought, how optimistic everyone was when the sun was shining, and how much they all hoped for a lovely summer. But at the same time, nobody could help expecting the worst!

As she arrived home, she saw Anita getting out of a taxi. Anita had been shopping too.

'Although it's a sin to be in the shops on such a nice day,' she remarked. 'I feel like I should be jogging around the block or something.'

Pippa grinned. Both she and Anita agreed that jogging was the most boring thing in the world.

'I'm thinking of having a barbecue tonight,' she told Anita. 'Would you like to come?'

'Love to.' Anita nodded cheerfully. 'Thanks.'

Pippa rang around the rest of her friends. Lissa was visiting her mum in Croydon and couldn't make it, but Pam and Jane said they'd be delighted to come if they could bring their boyfriends too. Pippa liked Eric and Steve and said she'd love to see them. Sherry, her other friend, texted back to say that a barbecue sounded great.

Pippa then went to the local twenty-four-hour store and bought some steaks, vegetables and potatoes. She also bought a few bottles of wine, which she put straight into the fridge. Then she went outside and lit the barbecue. By the time her friends had all arrived, it was glowing gently.

'This was a great idea,' said Anita as Pippa

brought out the meat and salads as well as wine and glasses.

'Let me,' said Pam's boyfriend, Eric, as Pippa unwrapped the meat.

'I can manage,' Pippa told him.

'Please let him.' Pam grinned at her. 'You know what men are like with fire and food.'

Pippa laughed but allowed Eric to put the meat on the grill.

Soon the smell of the barbecue wafted around the garden. Hobo wandered over, looking for his share.

'Honestly, that cat eats better than either of us,' said Anita as she gave Hobo a morsel of steak. 'And you'd swear he was a dog, the way he packs it in.'

They sat on the chairs that Pippa had brought out from the flat and tucked in to the food. Pippa enjoyed nights like this with her friends, although part of her still missed Mark. Especially when the other girls were there with their boyfriends. She wondered what the chances were of finding someone who wouldn't cheat on her next time.

'Hey, stop trying to steal my food!' Sherry poked Hobo with her toe. 'Here, chase this!'

She picked up the crumpled sheet of drawing paper that Pippa had thrown at Hobo the night before and which had ended up under the rose bush. But in the end she didn't throw it. She opened it out instead.

'Who's this?' she asked her friend as she looked at the sketch.

'Oh . . . nobody.' Pippa blushed.

'Nobody?' Sherry raised an eyebrow. 'A very attractive nobody.'

'Let's see.' Pam grabbed the paper and soon they were all looking at Pippa's drawing.

'Come on,' said Anita. 'Who is he?'

Pippa sighed. Then she told them about him sitting down at her table near the canal, and how she'd seen him again at the hotel while she was checking out.

'He's hunky,' agreed Jane. 'But why did you draw him?'

'I couldn't help it,' admitted Pippa. 'He sort of got into my head, and then I saw him again in Luton.'

'Really?'

'Yes. He was coming out of one of the offices where I had a meeting.'

'A weird coincidence.'

'That's what I thought too,' said Pippa.

'Maybe it's fate,' Anita told her cheerfully. 'Maybe your destiny is with this man.'

'Oh, knock it off,' snorted Steve, Jane's

boyfriend. 'You girls are all the same. You see a man and straightaway you think true love and destiny and rubbish like that.'

'Hey!' Jane shoved him. 'You'd be so lucky to think I was in love with you.'

Steve looked sheepish. 'Sorry,' he said.

'You're getting into hot water there, mate,' said Eric.

Pippa laughed. 'I don't think it's destiny or fate,' she said, 'but it was odd seeing him again, and he has a very attractive face.'

'I didn't realise you could draw so well,' said Anita.

'It relaxes me,' said Pippa. 'I often draw pictures of my customers. Helps me to remember them. Though I like doing pictures of Hobo best.'

Anita laughed. 'Don't say that,' she told her. 'It makes you sound like a sad single girl living with a cat and no boyfriend. We all know that you don't want to end up like that!'

Later that night, as Pippa lay in bed, she wondered about men. She wondered why most women thought having a boyfriend was so important. Even successful women like Anita. She wondered why she and her friends complained about men so much but got so upset when they split up with them. Why meeting a new man was always an occasion for great excitement. Why people felt a bit sorry for you when you said you weren't seeing anyone. What was it about having someone in your life, thought Pippa, that made you feel differently about things too?

The truth was that she'd been much better off this last year without anyone. It had been nice to be able to do what she wanted without having to think about someone else's feelings, but sometimes . . . She sighed. She had to be honest and say that sometimes she wished there was a man in her life. She missed going for a drink with a man, or laughing with him over dinner, and she missed the closeness, too.

It was seeing that guy beside the canal that had got her thinking like this. There had been something about him, something that had made her want to know him, which was really silly, because she'd hardly spoken two words to him. And yet . . .

I wouldn't have given him a second thought, Pippa told herself, if I hadn't seen him again at the hotel. Or maybe it's because of Luton. I'm thinking about him because of that, not because of anything else. Not because when I close my eyes I can still smell his aftershave.

She pulled the sheet over her shoulders. Aftershave! She was going bonkers, she really was. She should stop having silly thoughts and think about next week at work instead.

Chapter Four

Pippa was first in to the office on Monday morning. She looked through her list of potential customers and new customers and made a plan of who she was going to visit. She decided that this week she would concentrate on Liverpool and the surrounding area. She liked Liverpool. She liked the people.

'Do you want to come to dinner with me when you're here?' asked Lily Carr, one of her oldest clients. 'Unless you have something else planned?'

'Dinner would be great!'

Pippa was delighted. Lily had been a customer of Defender for over five years and the two of them got on well together. Pippa's first sale had been to Lily, although she hadn't told her that until the contract was signed. Lily had laughed and said that the security system had been the first thing she'd bought for the company, because she'd only been promoted the week before. A bond had developed between the two girls after that and they kept in touch.

Even though Lily and Pippa talked about business, they also talked about their lives. Lily had been sympathetic when Pippa and Mark had split up. Pippa had been equally sympathetic when Lily and her ex-husband had separated. More sympathetic, really, because the end of a marriage was worse than just splitting up with a boyfriend.

'Oh, it was a mistake from the start,' Lily told her. 'We were just too young. To be honest, I think my head was turned by the idea of a wedding.'

'Really?'

'Yes,' Lily said. 'Lots of my friends were getting married and I wanted the white dress and the lacy veil and the huge party too.'

'Not great reasons for getting married.'

'No.' Then Lily had laughed. 'But it sure was a great wedding.'

It was now over a year since Lily's divorce and she was dating a new man. She told Pippa all about him when they met for dinner at an Italian restaurant around the corner from Lily's office.

It was a small, old-fashioned restaurant. The walls were hung with brightly coloured paintings of Italy and the floor was covered in big, uneven terracotta tiles. There were tubs of flowers dotted around the room. The background music was soft and low.

Pippa and Lily both ordered steaming plates of penne and spicy tomato sauce. The waiter had also brought plenty of garlic bread, which Pippa loved. Both girls had asked for a glass of red wine too.

'His name is Kevin,' said Lily. 'He's a dentist.'

'Ugh!' Pippa made a face. 'I don't know how anyone can spend their time looking into other people's mouths.'

'Me neither,' confessed Lily, 'but he likes it and he's always busy.'

'Is he your dentist?' asked Pippa. 'Did you meet him lying back in his chair with your mouth open? Did he think you were coming on to him?'

Lily laughed. 'No,' she said. 'I met him at the gym. At a spinning class.'

'That sounds far too healthy,' said Pippa as she reached for another slice of garlic bread. I wouldn't want to meet the man of my dreams tonight, she thought as she bit into it. The stink of garlic off my breath would send him away in an instant!

'I don't go to the gym that often,' admitted Lily, 'but I'd put on a stone after my marriage broke up. Comfort eating, I suppose. I kept snacking on Kit Kats and Mars bars. The result of it ended up on my hips and my belly,' she added.

Pippa grinned. 'You look great now.'

'Thanks,' said Lily. 'I've lost eleven pounds. Maybe it'll all go horribly wrong if I split up with Kevin, but at the moment he's doing wonders for me in a whole heap of ways.'

'I'm glad to hear it.' Pippa was still grinning.

'And so how about you?' asked Lily. 'Anyone on the horizon?'

Pippa was about to shrug her shoulders and say no when the door of the restaurant opened. She glanced up and gasped, because the man who had walked into the restaurant was the same man she'd seen in Birmingham. The man who'd been at the canal and who'd been staying at the Hyatt hotel. The man who'd been in Luton as well.

This was beyond spooky, thought Pippa. It really was.

He was dressed down again. He was wearing a grey T-shirt and faded jeans and had a light jacket slung over his shoulder. He was looking around for a free table. For a moment his blue eyes met Pippa's brown ones. He frowned slightly. She looked away.

'Hey, Pippa, is everything OK?' Lily was staring at her.

34

'Oh, yes, fine.'

'Only you seemed to go off into a daze.'

'Yes.' Pippa shook her head. 'Sorry.'

'Is something the matter?'

'No,' said Pippa. 'It's just . . .'

'What?'

The waiter had shown the man to a seat near the window. He was now sitting down and studying the menu.

'What?' asked Lily again.

'Don't turn around,' said Pippa.

Lily turned around straightaway.

'Lily!'

'What?'

'It's that guy,' said Pippa. 'The one by himself near the window.'

'He's very good-looking,' said Lily. 'I don't blame you for fancying him.'

'I don't fancy him!' Pippa said, a little too loudly. A girl at the next table glanced across at them.

'I don't fancy him,' said Pippa again, more quietly. 'I don't even know him, but I keep seeing him.'

'What do you mean?' Lily was interested.

'He keeps turning up in the same places as me,' said Pippa.

'Like where?'

Pippa explained about having seen him in Birmingham, and again in Luton. Lily looked puzzled.

'Do you think he's following you?' she asked.

'I don't know,' said Pippa. She shook her head. 'It can't be very likely, can it? After all, it was just by chance I saw him at the restaurant. And I suppose he had to stay somewhere in the city, so why wouldn't it be the Hyatt? It's just – Luton too? And now here? That's really strange.'

Lily nodded. 'He's a bit of all right, isn't he?'

'Lily!'

'Well, he is,' said Lily. 'If I kept seeing a mystery man, I'd rather it was one like him than a slob.'

Pippa giggled. 'I suppose so.'

'He seems to be on his own,' said Lily. 'He's ordering food.'

'He was on his own in Birmingham too.'

'Perhaps he's a salesperson. Like you.'

'Perhaps.'

'In fact, he probably is,' said Lily. 'He has a briefcase and he's reading through notes. I bet you do that when you're on your own.'

'Sometimes,' admitted Pippa.

'I wonder what he sells.'

'Office supplies,' suggested Pippa.

'Water coolers,' said Lily.

'Telephone systems,' said Pippa.

'Maybe he's a banker,' said Lily. 'Maybe he goes around meeting customers.'

'Or maybe he just stocks up the machines in the bathrooms,' said Pippa.

Lily laughed. So did Pippa.

The man looked briefly in their direction. Then he returned to his notes, and the girls turned their attention to their food.

Chapter Five

The next day Pippa drove to Manchester for another set of meetings, but things didn't go as well as she'd expected.

Two prospective clients had already signed contracts with Safety Net and weren't interested in Defender. Pippa frowned when she heard the news. Tessa Bond, in Luton, had been considering Safety Net too. It was a new company and the people in Manchester told her that it was offering free twenty-four-hour phone assistance. Pippa wasn't sure that many people would need someone to talk to them at any time, night or day, but she understood that it sounded good.

She was worried about the fact that the Safety Net rep seemed to have been to every company before her and that everyone was excited about phone assistance twenty-four hours a day. She was also annoyed because the rep had called Defender 'dated'.

'Defender has been in business for over twenty years,' she told the manager who'd said this to her. 'We understand computer security, and we upgrade our software all the time.'

'Safety Net has twenty-four-hour personal phone support,' said the manager.

Pippa gritted her teeth. This phone support gimmick was really starting to annoy her.

'Nobody needs that,' she said.

'We do,' said the manager. 'We often work late at night.'

'You can get online support from us,' Pippa said. 'You don't need phone support too.'

'I like talking to real people,' said the manager. 'I hate sending emails when I have problems. I don't know for sure they're going to be answered.'

'I promise you, Defender replies to every one.'

'Well, I'm going with the phone support.'

The manager had clearly made his mind up. Pippa tried to smile as she told him she understood perfectly. Then she said that if he ever needed any help to call her.

'I don't need to,' the manager said. 'I'll get what I need from Safety Net.'

She left the office in a temper. She was still annoyed when she went to her next meeting. She was even more annoyed to discover that they already had the Safety Net system in place.

This visit wasn't going at all well. She'd never

been in this sort of situation before. Her chances of winning Salesperson of the Year and the all-expenses-paid trip to New York suddenly seemed to be slipping away from her.

The last meeting was in a glass office building near the city centre. Pippa had arranged her day so that her final call would leave her within walking distance of her hotel. She wanted to be able to go back to her room and chill out for a while. She'd also expected to be celebrating a few new customers, but things weren't working out like that.

She took a deep breath as she walked into the reception area of the office building and asked for Peter Smith, the manager of the company she was visiting. She'd spoken to Peter a few times on the phone and she thought she got on well with him.

The receptionist told her to take the lift to the tenth floor. Peter would meet her there, she said.

Pippa got into the lift. She checked her hair in the mirror and tugged at her navy skirt to make it smoother. She'd just finished adding some gloss to her lips when the doors opened.

'Hello, Pippa,' said Peter Smith. 'Nice to see you.'

'Hello, Peter,' she replied. 'Good of you to take the time to meet me.'

He led her into his office. It was large and bright and looked over the city.

'Great view,' she said.

'I think so too,' he told her.

'Right.' She wanted to get down to business straightaway. 'Let's talk about your security needs.'

She explained about Defender's security programme and offered to break into the company's computer system. Peter Smith smiled at her.

'You're right, of course,' he said. 'It's far too easy to hack into our system. Someone did it already today.'

'No!' She looked horrified.

'It was part of a demo too,' Peter said.

'What sort of demo?' Pippa was getting a bad feeling.

'Of another software security programme,' said Peter.

'Don't tell me.' Pippa gritted her teeth. 'Safety Net.'

Peter looked surprised.

'Yes,' he said. 'Their salesman was here earlier. He explained about their system and how it works. And that there's twenty-four-hour phone support.'

'I know,' said Pippa.

41

'The thing is,' said Peter, 'they're offering a great deal.'

'I'm sure they are,' she said, 'but let's talk about what Defender does first.'

She gave it her very best shot. She talked about the way the software protected the computer system. She talked about the benefits Peter's company would have. She went into every single detail she could and showed the system to him in her company's glossy brochure.

'And so,' she said finally, 'I think you have to agree that Defender is the best bet for your business.'

Peter Smith looked doubtful.

'I can see it's top notch,' he agreed, 'but maybe it's a bit too top notch for us.'

'Of course it's not,' she protested.

'It's certainly too expensive.'

This was what the other people she'd visited recently had said too. Nobody had ever complained about the cost of Defender before.

'I'm sure we can work something out,' she said.

'I need to think about it,' said Peter Smith. 'I'm going to look at both proposals and decide next week.'

'That's fine.' Pippa smiled at him, even

though inside she was fuming. 'Take all the time you need, and if you have any other questions, please call me.'

'I will,' said Peter.

He saw her as far as the lift. She got inside and pressed the button for the ground floor. When she was outside the building, she took out her mobile phone and rang Richard in the office. She told him about Safety Net and the twenty-four-hour phone support. She said that it was a big problem, and that they'd have to come up with something themselves.

'If one of our support people has to call around to our customers with cups of coffee and biscuits, then that's what we need to do,' she told Richard. 'Because otherwise we're toast!'

'Let me think about it,' said Richard. 'In the meantime, you have to get out there and meet as many people as you can before the Safety Net guy gets to them.'

Easier said than done, Pippa thought. How was she to know where the Safety Net rep was going next? And how would she manage to get there before him?

Chapter Six

When Pippa got back to the hotel, she went up to her room and kicked off her high-heeled shoes. She rubbed her feet for a few minutes. Then lay down on the bed and closed her eyes, but even though she was tired, she couldn't sleep. She was fretting about Safety Net and Defender and her customers, and she was fretting about the all-expenses-paid trip to New York too.

After a while she got up from the bed and changed out of her suit and into jeans and a T-shirt. She went downstairs to the lounge area and ordered some bar food. Usually she didn't eat in the hotels where she stayed, but she was still tired and didn't feel like going out. Besides, the Thai chicken with noodles looked good, and it was one of her favourite dishes.

When Pippa had finished eating, she opened the newspaper she'd bought earlier in the day. The news was always more cheerful in the summer, but today's main story was about a politician making false expenses claims. She shook her head slowly. She couldn't understand how it was that people in power still seemed to make such incredible 'mistakes'. The politician had said the claim for a family holiday had been a 'mistake'. Pippa knew that if she handed in unusual expenses claims to Richard, he'd spot it straightaway. He wouldn't let her make such a 'mistake'. She smiled to herself. Maybe Defender could develop a programme for government departments to check expenses. That would be a good contract to get.

She sat back in her chair and imagined having to go to Westminster to see someone about buying a Defender system. It would be fun, and a challenge. She was sure she could do it.

Maybe they needed something like that to make up for the fact that Safety Net seemed to be stealing all her customers!

As she thought about walking through the corridors of power, she looked across the lounge and her eyes opened even wider. She couldn't believe what she saw. Walking towards her was the man from Birmingham. From Luton. And from Liverpool too.

This was too much. It couldn't be a coincidence. She shifted uneasily in her seat. Was he following her? If so, why?

He walked straight past her and towards the

bar. He didn't seem to have noticed her at all, which wasn't exactly what she would have expected from somebody who was following her. Maybe, she thought, he was trying to put her off the scent.

Then he suddenly turned around and looked straight at her. His expression was surprised. She could see that he recognised her.

'It's you again,' he said. 'What on earth are you doing here?'

'What do you mean?' she demanded. 'I should be asking you the same thing.'

'I can't believe it,' he said. 'I saw you in a restaurant in Birmingham, and one in Liverpool. Now you're here too! Are you following me?'

'Me? Following you?' She looked astonished. 'It's you who's following me.'

'Not at all,' he said. 'You're one step behind me all the time. Now that I think about it, you were in Luton too, weren't you? I remember now. You were in the reception area of a company I visited. I thought there was something vaguely familiar about you, but I didn't know what it was. I was there before you. So you were following me.'

He had a point, Pippa knew, but she also knew that she wasn't following him.

'What about the Hyatt in Birmingham?' she said. 'Didn't you see me there?'

He looked startled.

'So you *are* following me,' he said. 'Why? What do you want?'

'Oh, don't be so silly,' she told him. 'I'm definitely not following you. I was staying at the Hyatt and I saw you there. It was when I was checking out. So were you.'

'I don't remember,' he said.

'Well, I do,' she told him.

'I was there on business,' he said.

'So was I.'

He looked at her for a moment and she felt herself blush. He was still wearing his suit and tie, but her jeans and T-shirt weren't very businesslike. Not that she needed to be looking businesslike now. All the same, she looked more like a tourist than a successful salesperson. She wished that she was wearing her decent shoes at least, but she'd slid her feet into her comfortable flip-flops when she'd changed.

'And what business are you in?' he asked. 'Are you a spy?'

Pippa spluttered. 'What?'

'Trying to find out company secrets. If you are, you're not a very good one.'

'Don't be so silly,' said Pippa. 'I'm not a spy.'

'So why are you following me?'

'I'm not!' she cried. 'You're here on business. I'm here on business. It's a coincidence.'

He looked doubtful. Then, quite suddenly, he smiled.

'Tell you what,' he suggested. 'As we keep on bumping into each other, why don't you join me for a drink? Maybe that way we can solve the mystery.'

'I don't know . . .' Pippa wasn't sure that she wanted to have a drink with someone who thought she was a spy. He could be a stalker for all she knew.

He shrugged. As he did so, Pippa suddenly remembered that he was very hunky, with a nice smile. She realised that she didn't want to spend an evening by herself yet again. Maybe having a drink with a good-looking man in a public bar wasn't such a bad idea after all.

'Look, I'm sorry,' she said quickly. 'I was being rude. I'd be delighted to have a drink with you. Thank you.'

He smiled at her, and his blue eyes – his very sexy blue eyes – twinkled.

'What can I get you?' he asked.

'A glass of white wine,' she replied.

'OK.' He turned back towards the bar.

She looked at him. He was just as good-looking from behind, she thought. He had a good build; tall, athletic and a nice bum. She blushed as she thought about it. Just as well she was looking at his bum and not the other way around. Hers was a bit too wide for comfort. Or maybe, she told herself, it was wide for comfort!

She folded the newspaper and ran her fingers through her hair. Then she opened her handbag and discreetly sprayed her neck and wrists with her Kenzo perfume. She also added some more gloss to her lips.

He returned from the bar with a bottle of beer and her glass of wine. Then he sat down in the leather chair opposite her.

'Cheers,' she said, raising the glass towards him. 'Thank you.'

'You're welcome.' He smiled at her again. 'It's nice to see you.'

'Really?'

'Yes,' he said. 'I don't know about you, but I get bored and lonely when I'm travelling. It's good to see a familiar face, even though I don't know who you are!'

She agreed with him. Her friends never really understood how dull being on the road could be sometimes. They would tell her that she was lucky not to work office hours, and lucky to stay in nice hotels and have her meals paid for too. They were right about that, of course, but they never realised that it could be lonely. Or that sometimes she would have preferred to be home in front of the telly, eating food she'd cooked herself.

'My name's Gerry,' he said.

'Pippa.'

'Nice to meet you, Pippa,' he said. 'You know, when you gave me your table in Birmingham, I was going to ask if you wanted to join me for a drink, but I thought it would seem very rushed and cheeky. Then when you left I was annoyed with myself for not asking.'

'Oh.' Pippa was surprised. She hadn't expected to hear him say that.

'I thought you seemed very nice,' he said.

She grinned. 'Thanks.'

'So.' He settled back in his seat. 'Why are we following each other around the country?'

'I've no idea,' said Pippa.

'Well . . .' he began, but broke off as the fire alarm sounded.

Everyone in the lounge looked around uncertainly, and then the staff told them all to leave the building. Pippa stood up and Gerry took her by the hand. His grasp was warm and dry.

He led her out of the bar and into the street, where a small crowd had already gathered. They stood and looked up at the hotel. There was nothing to see. Then they heard the sound of sirens, and a red fire engine pulled up at the pavement outside.

Two firemen got down from their engine, and then the onlookers saw the fire. It was in an enclosed yard beside the hotel, but the flames were now reaching up over the high wall.

'Wow!' cried Pippa as there was a bang and a shower of sparks. The flames shot towards the sky.

Gerry gripped her hand a little more tightly.

The firemen began to unwind a hose and point it at the flames.

'We probably didn't need to leave the hotel,' said Gerry as they began to bring the fire under control. 'I suppose it's better to be safe than sorry.'

'Well, I guess management wouldn't be too happy if their guests got charred,' said Pippa.

Gerry laughed.

It was a further fifteen minutes before they were allowed back into the hotel.

'Would you like another glass of wine?' asked Gerry as they sat down at their table again. 'That one's probably a bit warm by now.'

'At least it's not because it got heated by the flames,' said Pippa. 'Another glass would be nice, thanks.'

The barman replaced their drinks for free.

'Though I wouldn't have minded paying,' said Gerry. 'It was quite exciting really.'

'Only because it wasn't serious.' Pippa shivered suddenly.

'True,' he said. ' I like to give a girl an exciting time on a first date.'

She smiled at him. 'It's hardly a date, but it's certainly been more exciting than I expected.'

'Would you like something to eat?' asked Gerry. 'Would that help it seem like more of a date?'

'I've had the Thai chicken already so I'm not hungry,' she told him. 'But if you need food, go ahead. Mine was great.'

'It might be a bit rude . . .'

'Of course it wouldn't be rude,' she said. 'Besides, I'm not sure I could cope with you fainting from lack of food.'

'OK then.' He raised his hand and ordered the chicken. 'Because you liked it,' he said.

She laughed. 'The pressure! The pressure! What will I do if you don't?'

He laughed too, and she realised that she was having fun with him.

'I know you've been travelling around, like me,' she said, 'but where are you from?'

'London,' he replied. 'Camden.'

'I'm in Shepherd's Bush.'

'Not too far away,' he said happily. 'So we might get together again?'

'Maybe,' she said.

'Only maybe?' He looked disappointed.

'Well . . .'

'How long are you staying here in Manchester?' he asked.

'Until tomorrow.'

'So what job has you travelling around the country?'

'Computers,' she said casually. She never told anyone she was a sales rep. People were funny about sales reps. They always seemed to think she was going to try selling stuff to them straightaway. 'How about you?'

'I'm a consultant,' he said.

'A doctor?' Her eyes widened. She wished she had a doctor like him. Her own doctor, although friendly, certainly wasn't good-looking.

'No,' he said. 'Business. Though I'd like to be a rock star.'

She laughed.

'Honestly,' he told her. His face was serious. 'My friends all want me to go on *Britain's Got Talent*.'

'You're joking!'

'No,' he said, and then grinned. 'They want me to go on it because I can't sing for nuts. They want to see me make a fool of myself.'

'Not very nice friends,' said Pippa.

'They think it would do me good,' he said. 'They think that I take life too seriously.'

Pippa didn't say that her friends thought the same about her. She smiled at him. She was beginning to feel comfortable in his company.

As they chatted together, she discovered that, like her, Gerry often listened to country music when he was driving.

'I never tell anyone that usually,' said Pippa. 'It seems so uncool.'

'It can be our guilty secret,' Gerry told her. 'Don't you dare tell anyone that I once had a poster of Shania Twain on my wall.'

'You didn't!'

'I did, but I was younger then. Besides, she's a hot lady. I like women in denim.' He grinned. 'I liked the skirt you were wearing in Birmingham.'

Pippa blushed. It had been her shortest because the weather had been so warm.

'So do you have to travel much as a consultant?' she asked. She didn't want to talk about hot women and short skirts. Not yet, anyway.

'A fair bit,' replied Gerry. 'We're on a big push at the moment, so I'm going all over the place. I'm in Stoke-on-Trent tomorrow.'

The little knot that had been forming for a while in Pippa's tummy eased. She wasn't going to Stoke-on-Trent the next day. She was going to Sheffield. He wasn't following her.

'I'm not going there,' she said happily. 'So we're not following each other around after all. It was just chance that we were in the same places.'

Suddenly his phone rang. He looked annoyed as he took it out of his pocket. He made a face as he said hello to the caller.

'What's up, Sam?' he said.

He listened for a moment, then spoke again.

'But I thought the contracts were e-mailed to them . . . I thought they were going to sign . . . Yes, I know . . . but . . .' He sighed.

Pippa looked around her while he was talking. She didn't want to listen to his conversation although she couldn't really help hearing parts of it. He was getting very annoyed with Sam, whoever Sam was.

In the end, Gerry snapped his phone closed and got up.

'I'm really sorry,' he said. 'I have to go and do some work.'

'That's a shame,' she told him.

'I enjoyed talking to you.'

'Me too.'

'When do you get back to London?'

'Probably at the weekend,' she said.

'Can I call you?' he asked.

She felt her heart flutter. The hunk wanted to call her. He hadn't been bored by her.

'Well . . . yes, sure.' She couldn't help the shiver of excitement that suddenly ran through her body. 'That would be great.'

They exchanged mobile numbers, then Pippa stood up.

'Good night,' she said.

Gerry leaned forward slightly and gave her a kiss on the cheek. The shiver ran through her again.

'Thanks for the drink,' she said.

'Thanks for the company,' he told her. 'Are you off anywhere exciting next?'

'No,' she said. 'Just meeting more clients. It's all go in the computer world.'

'I bet it is.' He nodded. 'Well . . . it was nice meeting you.'

'You too,' said Pippa. 'So . . . good night.'

'Good night.'

She walked across the lobby. Then she looked back. He was watching her. She pressed the button for the lift, stepped inside and leaned against the wall as it brought her gently up to the tenth floor.

Chapter Seven

It had been a very busy week, and Pippa woke up late on Saturday morning. She'd fallen into a deep sleep when she got into bed. Her dreams had been mixed, but she knew that Gerry featured in them. He'd featured in all of her dreams since she'd met him.

He'd texted her over a dozen times since Liverpool. Short messages, just to say hello. To tell her to turn on her radio and listen to a Johnny Cash special. To wish her good night. She smiled at the messages, although she hadn't listened to Johnny Cash. She'd been at a meeting when the radio show was on. The night-time texts had been nice. It was lovely to know someone was thinking about her as she was climbing into bed.

He also texted to say that he hoped they could meet up in London. She hoped so too. She'd never felt so attracted to anyone else in her life before. She kept telling herself not to get carried away. He was only a man, and he'd probably break her heart. They all did sooner or later, but she couldn't help it. She really liked him. She fancied him a lot and she definitely wanted to see him again.

They hadn't made an actual date. Gerry had said that he wasn't sure what time he'd get home. He said he'd call her. Pippa leaned out of her bed and picked up her mobile. There were no texts and no missed calls. She looked at her watch. It was after eleven in the morning. Was he going to call? Or was she really only his reserve night out? The person to call if his other plans didn't happen?

She got out of bed and opened her yellow curtains. Rubbing her eyes in the bright sunlight, she went into the bathroom. She got into the shower and stood under the stream of water. She poured shampoo into her hand and rubbed it through her hair. An aroma of coconut floated in the air. Soon it was joined by the scent of oranges. Pippa liked her fruity-smelling shampoos and shower soaps. Last Christmas her older brother, Bill, had given her a lovely set of soaps, shampoos and creams. She was still working her way through them all.

She spent a long time in the bathroom and nearly as long again drying her hair. It always took ages because it was thick and curly. That was why she wore it in a bun when she was on the road. Keeping it up meant she didn't have to wash it those mornings and it saved her time.

When she'd finished drying her hair, she checked her mobile again. She didn't know whether she'd call Gerry if he hadn't called her, but he had. Typical, she thought, that he would phone when she was in the shower! She rang her voice mail and listened to the message he'd left.

'Hi, Pippa,' he said. 'I didn't want to ring too early in case you were asleep. I forgot to ask if you were a morning person or a night person. Well, look . . . I was hoping you were OK to meet up? Today? Let me know.'

He'd sent her a text as well, which said the same thing.

She realised that she had a big smile on her face as she read it.

She dialled his number.

'Hi,' said Gerry.

'Hi,' she said.

'You got my message?'

'Yes.'

'Silly question. Of course you got my message. You wouldn't be ringing otherwise.'

'You never know. I might be the sort of girl who likes ringing up strange men for no reason.'

'That's true, but I didn't get that impression.'

'What impression did you get?'

'That you were sweet and lovely.'

She laughed out loud. Nobody had ever called her sweet and lovely before. Not Mark, not any of her other boyfriends, not even her mum. Her mum usually called her headstrong and stubborn, although she said it with a smile.

'You've a lot to learn about me,' she told Gerry.

'I know. And I'm dying to start.'

'You are?'

'Absolutely. So . . . are you back in London?'

'Yes.'

'And would you like to meet today?'

She waited for a moment. She didn't want to sound too keen.

'Yes, I would,' she said.

'Great. Where would you like to go? When would you like to meet? This afternoon?'

She hadn't thought about meeting in the afternoon. She'd supposed they'd go on a date. To a pub or a restaurant, maybe. She didn't know what she could possibly do with him in the afternoon. Or . . . well . . . she did, but she wasn't planning to get into bed with him right away. Was that what he wanted?

'Well . . .' she said.

'I know it sounds corny, but it's such a lovely day I was wondering if you'd like to go on the London Eye,' he said. 'The views will be great and it's a fun thing to do.'

The London Eye! He was right. It *was* corny, but at least he wasn't saying that he wanted her to come to his flat. It wasn't that she wouldn't enjoy making love to him, of course, but there had to be a bit of mystery. That was what everyone said. They told her that she was too open, told people too much.

'That sounds great,' she said.

'Will I meet you there?' he asked.

'I guess so, yes.'

'About three?'

'Make it four,' she said.

'Oh. OK.' He sounded a little disappointed.

'See you later,' she told him.

'I can't wait,' he said.

Pippa went out and did some grocery shopping. Fruit, bread, milk and a large bar of chocolate. She bought bathroom stuff too, like loo cleaner and toilet rolls. She wanted to have a very un-romantic morning, so that the afternoon would be completely different.

She'd thought that the shopping would use up a few hours, but it only took forty minutes.

Afterwards she came home and made herself some coffee. She drank it sitting in the garden with Hobo the cat at her feet. When she'd finished, she took out her drawing pad and did another sketch of Gerry. She looked at it critically when she'd finished. She wondered if she'd made him a little too handsome. Was her memory playing tricks on her? She closed her drawing book. This time she didn't crumple up Gerry's picture. She went inside and put it on her desk.

She started to get ready early. She tried on her favourite jeans and T-shirts, but it was hot and she didn't want to be sweating beside him. So she decided on one of the new skirts and tops she'd bought a week earlier. The skirt had shades of orange and purple in it and the top was purple too. At first she'd been afraid that they'd clash with her hair, but purple suited her, and the orange made them summery. She wore her skirt and top with a pair of sandals that Lissa had made her buy in a market. They were comfortable sandals but very pretty. They had a low heel and coloured beads and so they went with almost everything. She also wore her favourite gold earrings and a selection of gold bracelets. The bracelets jangled whenever she moved. (The earrings were real gold, but the bracelets were just painted. She told herself that if she won the trip to New York, she'd buy some in real gold. As a present to herself for being the best salesperson in her company.)

Pippa hardly ever wore make-up at the weekend. Today, however, she dusted some bronzer on her face. It caught the rays of the sun and made her glow. She put mascara on her eyelashes and gloss on her lips. Then she sprayed herself with her Kenzo perfume.

She looked at herself in the mirror before she went out of the flat. She looked good. Her eyes were sparkling. Nearly as much as when she'd won the weekend in Paris for being the Salesperson of the Year.

She saw Gerry in Jubilee Gardens, which bustled with tourists and Londoners all enjoying the sunny weather. He was standing with his back to her, looking towards the river. He was back in his cargo pants and T-shirt combo and his hands were in his pockets. He looked relaxed and casual and he turned around just as she approached him.

'I sensed you there.' He smiled at her.

'Really?'

He nodded. He leaned forward as though he was going to kiss her, but suddenly stopped. He smiled again.

'I've got the tickets already.'

'Oh, right,' she said.

'You look lovely,' he told her.

'Thanks.'

'Those colours really suit you.'

She felt that she should pay him a compliment in return, but all she could think of was that he had great legs.

'I like your T-shirt,' she said lamely, and he laughed.

He took her by the hand and led her across the grass towards the Eye. Pippa had been on it when she'd first come to London, but the day hadn't been as clear and bright so the views had been a little disappointing.

Gerry had bought fast-track tickets, and they were soon in a capsule along with some excited, chattering European tourists. All of the tourists had cameras and they started taking photographs straightaway. Pippa rested her hand on the rail and looked at the Thames through the huge windows.

'London's fabulous, isn't it?' Gerry stood close beside her. She was very aware of his hand on the rail, almost touching hers. 'The most fabulous city in the world.'

She nodded. It was true. There was nowhere quite like it.

'Big Ben.' He was pointing out landmarks. 'St Paul's.'

She smiled. It was as though she was a tourist herself.

He put his arm around her.

She felt dizzy. She wasn't sure if it was because of his touch, or if it was because she didn't really like heights.

'I took a Thames cruise once,' he told her.

'Was it fun?'

'Not really,' he said. 'It was a work thing, with customers. You know, entertaining them. It's hard work keeping customers happy. Though I suppose you don't have to worry about that in your computer world.'

She was going to correct him and tell him that she didn't make computers. She didn't write software. She just sold stuff. But she didn't want to spoil the moment.

'This is much more enjoyable.' He leaned a little closer. 'It's so much nicer doing things with someone you like.'

He was so right. She was having a good time with him. She continued to gaze out of the window at the skyline of the city. Then they moved so that they were looking towards Tower Bridge.

'I think of the past when I look at it,' Gerry

told her. 'I think of the kings and queens of England; of Henry the Eighth and his six wives; of the treason and the plots.'

'Goodness,' she said. 'I didn't realise you were a history buff.'

'I'm not really,' he admitted. 'But you can't look at all this and not think about everything that happened.'

She nodded. She'd been thinking the same thing. It was weird how he seemed to be able to match her thoughts.

They watched the city in silence as the Eye made its circle. Then they got off together.

'I enjoyed that,' Pippa said.

'So did I.'

She glanced at her watch.

'Do you want to stroll upriver a little?' he asked.

'OK,' she said. She didn't really mind what they did. All she wanted was to be with him.

He bought a couple of ice creams from a nearby van. They were already melting as he brought them back. She licked at hers quickly so that it didn't drip on to her skirt.

'You've got some on your chin,' he told her. 'Just like the little girl over there.'

He nodded towards a family, where the smallest girl was eating an ice cream too. There was more of it on her face than anywhere else.

'I was never good at messy food,' Pippa told him as she wiped her chin.

'What *are* you good at?' he asked.

'Chips,' she said, and grinned at him.

They walked for a few minutes until they found a quieter spot. Then they sat down beside each other on the grass. He asked her about growing up in Bexley. He asked about her family. He asked about the holidays she'd been on and about her friends. She asked him the same sort of questions.

He'd grown up in Oxford, which, he said, was a lovely place to live. His parents were divorced. They'd split up when he was ten.

'I'm sorry,' she said.

'Oh, it wasn't a bad thing,' he told her. 'They weren't happy. Anyway, me and my two brothers stayed with Mum during the week and with Dad at weekends. Then he got married again. We didn't stay with him as much after that.'

'I guess that happens,' she said.

He nodded. 'I like Dad's new wife – well, not new now, of course. They've been together a long time.'

'Do they have children?'

'Two girls,' said Gerry.

'Do you see them often?'

'I don't see any of my family that often,' he said, 'but that's OK. It's not a big deal. I'm happy how things are. How about you? Do you go home much?'

'About once a month,' she said. 'I'll probably call by next weekend.'

'That's good timing,' he told her. 'Next weekend I'll be in Glasgow, so I won't be able to see you.'

She said nothing.

'Always supposing you want to see me again,' he added quickly.

'I'm thinking that I might,' she said. 'Only because you allow me to do things like eat ice cream before my dinner.'

He laughed, and so did she. Then he leaned towards her and kissed her, and she felt herself melt inside. Just like an ice cream in the sun.

Chapter Eight

They went to a bistro near Arlington Road for dinner. Pippa had been there a few times with her friends and she liked it. Although it was small, it was bright and cheerful, with white tables and multicoloured chairs. The food was good too.

They held hands as they walked inside. Mark had never held her hand in restaurants. He thought it was a sissy sort of thing to do.

Gerry and Pippa waited until one of the waiters came over to them and showed them to a table. He also brought them the menu, which was on a long card.

Pippa glanced at it and said that she'd have their spicy chicken with chips. Then she changed her mind and said that she'd have salad instead of chips. After all, she thought, if I'm going to have a new boyfriend, I want to keep slim.

'But the chips here are lovely,' protested Gerry.

'I know,' she said. 'I'm a big fan of chips, but salads are better for keeping off the pounds.'

'You look fine,' he said firmly. 'You're just right.'

Pippa felt herself blush. 'Thanks very much,' she said, 'but I'll still have the salad.'

'I'll have the burger,' said Gerry to the waiter. 'You can give me plenty of chips, because I bet she'll nick some of mine.'

Pippa laughed. 'I won't steal them. I promise.'

When the food arrived and the waiter put the golden chips in a bowl in front of Gerry, Pippa looked at them longingly.

'Go on,' he said, 'have one.'

'Just the one.' She popped a chip into her mouth. It was hot and floury and it tasted great. She smiled at him. 'Thanks.'

'Help yourself,' he told her.

'Don't tempt me.' She poured some oil on her salad. 'I'm not dieting. I'm just trying to be healthy.' She sighed. 'It's not always easy.'

'Especially when you have to travel a lot,' agreed Gerry. 'You can end up eating the most awful rubbish.'

'I try really hard not to,' she said.

'You don't need to worry about your weight,' he said. 'Besides, I hate stick-thin women.'

'I'll never be that.'

'Good.'

'Thanks for the trip on the Eye,' she said. 'It was fun.'

'I enjoyed it too,' he told her. 'It was my first time.'

She laughed. 'Not really?'

'Yes,' he said. 'That's the trouble with living in London. You never do the things that visitors do.'

'You're right,' she agreed, 'but I made a promise to myself to go to lots of different places after I was here for a while. So I've been to the Tate and to the Imperial War Museum and to Madame Tussauds . . .'

She didn't say that she'd done all these things on the days when she was feeling particularly lonely after her break-up with Mark.

'The Imperial War Museum,' he said. 'That's a bit bloodthirsty for a girl, surely?'

'Sexist beast.' She smiled at him. 'I love planes and machinery and all that sort of thing. The museum has cannons and everything in it.'

'You're a very surprising person, Pippa Jones.' He reached across the table and took her hand in his.

'And you're too sexy for your own good,' she said in return.

They sat looking into each other's eyes for a moment. Then the waiter returned to take away their empty plates.

'Dessert?' he asked.

Pippa said that she was stuffed, but Gerry ordered chocolate cheesecake.

'See, it's not just women who like chocolate,' he said, which made her giggle.

'I do like it,' she agreed. 'I just couldn't manage it.'

'Oh, I can eat for England,' he told her. 'When I was in France last year, they couldn't believe I was packing away so much food every night.'

'Where in France were you?' she asked. She thought he was going to say Paris. She was getting ready to say she'd been in Paris too.

Instead he told her that he'd been on an adventure holiday – white-water rafting.

'I did that as well!' She looked at him in surprise. 'Last summer. I was in Paris too, for a weekend, but my proper holiday was rafting.'

'Really?'

She nodded. 'The Verdon river.'

'You're joking.' He looked amazed. 'Me too.'

'When?'

'Beginning of June.'

'End of June.'

They looked at each other in amazement.

'So . . .' Gerry grinned at Pippa. 'We both like adventure holidays and we both secretly like country music and we both like chips – I'd say that has to be a good thing.'

73

'And we both like chocolate,' she reminded him as she stole the last morsel of cheesecake from his plate.

'Hey!' he laughed.

'Sorry.' She bit into it. 'I couldn't help myself. It was tempting me . . .'

'I wonder what *I* could tempt you to do,' he said.

She didn't reply.

'I'm sorry,' he said. 'Was I too obvious there?'

'A bit.'

'I'm not just trying to sleep with you, you know,' he told her. 'I like you. I want to . . . I want to go out with you.'

'You are out with me,' she said.

'I know. I want to do this again.'

'So do I,' she said.

He leaned across the table. She thought he was going to kiss her, but instead he wiped a chocolate crumb from her cheek.

It was still bright as they left the restaurant, although the air was starting to cool down. Gerry asked Pippa if she'd like to come back to his flat for a while. She looked at him doubtfully.

'Just for a drink,' he said. 'No pressure, Pippa.'

She never went back to men's houses or flats

on first dates. She just didn't. It gave them the wrong idea, but Gerry was different.

'One drink,' she said.

'Excellent!'

He held her hand again as they walked along the quiet streets. She liked walking hand-in-hand with him. He made her feel very safe.

'And here we are,' he said after ten minutes. 'My place.'

He lived in the basement part of an old house but, like her, he was lucky enough to have a small garden. As he led her through the flat to show her, she could see that it was neat and clean. Apart from a mound of unironed washing piled up on the sofa, and an equally high stack of newspapers piled up on the kitchen table.

'I'm terrible about the papers,' he said as he noticed her looking at them. 'I buy all of them every Sunday and I spend the week reading them. So by Friday I'm pretty much on old news.'

She laughed. 'Not a bad thing, sometimes.'

'No. Then, of course, when I'm driving around the place I don't get to read them at all. So sometimes I read about the major problem in the world and how it's been solved all in the one day.'

'I do the same,' she admitted. 'Although I only buy one paper.'

It was another thing they had in common, she thought. They were so alike it was almost frightening.

She looked out the window at his garden, which was smaller than hers. It was just a court-yard really, but it had lots of flowers in it.

'Green fingers too,' she said. 'I can't match that, though. I'm not great in the garden.'

'To be honest, neither am I,' he admitted. 'It was like this when I moved in. I just pull up weeds and hope for the best.'

'Nice,' she said. 'Mine is just grass.'

'But good to have open space in the city,' he said.

She nodded in agreement.

'Anyway. Drink. Do you want to sit inside? It's a bit chilly outside now.'

She sat at the table.

'What would you like?' he asked. 'Wine? Beer? Water? Spirits?'

'No more wine.' They'd shared a bottle over dinner and she knew it had made her light-headed. 'Do you have sparkling water?'

'Sure.' He opened the fridge and then tut-tutted. 'I forgot to get some. I'll pop out to the shop. I'll only be a minute.'

'No, no, it's OK,' she protested. 'I'll have a juice instead.'

'I don't have any juice either,' he said. 'I should've thought ... it's just that I've been away so much ...'

'Don't worry,' she said. 'I'm fine. Tap water will do.'

But no matter how much she said it was OK, he insisted on going out to get water for her.

'There's a corner shop at the end of the road,' he said. 'I'll be five minutes at the most.'

It was brave of him to leave her alone in his flat, she thought. There must be no secrets in his life.

The front door closed. Pippa was tempted to sneak around the flat and check it out, but she stopped herself. It wouldn't be right. Instead she sat down and looked at his pile of papers. *The Sunday Times* was on the top. She'd already read that. As she moved the papers to find one she hadn't read, the entire pile tipped over on to the floor.

'Bloody hell!' she cried.

There were lots of them. She picked them up and started putting them on the table again. Then she saw the brochure. It was a glossy brochure with a picture on the front of it. The picture was of a man, holding a computer, falling off a tightrope. Underneath was a big safety net, and beside the net was another picture. This time of Gerry. She stared at it.

It was an advertising brochure. The sort that she gave to her customers. Along the bottom it said: *Don't let your system crash! Make sure you have a Safety Net. Call us now.* Underneath was a phone number and an e-mail address.

Pippa knew that her mouth was open. She knew that her heart was beating faster in her chest. Gerry was a systems security sales person! Like her! But he'd called himself a consultant. Why had he tricked her like that?

She continued to look at the brochure. Another line read: Talk to our Security Sales Consultant, Gerry Williams.

She'd assumed he was some kind of trouble-shooter. That sort of a consultant. Not a sales consultant, which was what her official title was too.

That was why she'd kept bumping into him in the places that she visited! He was the one who'd been ahead of her in Manchester. He was the one whose company was offering twenty-four-hour phone support. He was the one who could do her out of her Salesperson of the Year award. And her trip to New York! Her hands shook.

Did he know? Had he guessed? Was he aware that she was his rival?

She sat down on the chair with a thump.

Of course he knew. Of course he'd guessed. That was why he'd talked to her in the first place. He'd been meeting her customers, hadn't he? He'd figured it out. He'd wanted to know where she was going after Manchester. She'd thought it was because he cared about her, but really it was so that he could get to prospective clients ahead of her. How lucky she hadn't told him about her plans. He'd probably only bought her a drink in the hopes of loosening her tongue. She was such a fool to think that he'd enjoyed her company. She blushed as she remembered chatting about her life and telling him about her love of country music. He'd probably only pretended to like it himself. He'd never had a poster of Shania Twain on his bedroom wall! The more she thought about him the more embarrassed she felt.

She got to her feet and grabbed her bag. She wasn't staying here to be made a fool of. She wasn't going to let him question her. She was going home right now. Before he returned. Before he had a chance to turn on his charm.

The charm that had made some of her prospective customers sign up with Safety Net instead of Defender. He knew what he was doing all right. Smarmy git! How could she have been such a fool?

Pippa hurried out of the flat and banged the door behind her before racing up the steps and looking each way. There was no sign of him. She ran across the road and down a side street out of sight.

She walked for about five minutes and then she saw a cab. She hailed it and jumped in. She'd just given the driver her address when her phone started to buzz. It was Gerry. She ignored it. Instead she blew her nose and wiped the tears from her cheeks. She'd nearly made a huge mistake. But she hadn't.

The only trouble was, instead of being happy about it, she felt as though she'd been punched in the stomach. All she wanted to do was curl up and cry.

Chapter Nine

When Pippa got back to her flat, she burst into tears. She couldn't believe she'd been taken for a ride. She should have guessed. Hunky men like Gerry didn't go out with girls like her. Men like Gerry went out with girls who looked like the celebrities in the glossy magazines. They went for girls with long blond hair and tanned bodies and fake nails. They went for those kinds of girls because they could, because they were good-looking enough to attract them. They went for models, not sales reps. Even if they were sales reps themselves.

How long had he known? When did he guess that she was his rival? In the hotel in Manchester where he'd bought her a drink? Or before that? In Birmingham? Maybe he had seen her at the Hyatt after all. Maybe he'd wondered about her in the casual way she'd wondered about him. Maybe he'd asked at reception and they'd said that she was there on business. Perhaps he'd found out who she worked for and decided to follow her to see what companies she was visiting, so that he could do deals and undercut her prices. Although, she remembered, wiping her eyes, he'd been ahead of her sometimes. But that could've been luck. Or guesswork. Whatever.

Her phone rang again. Gerry's name popped up. She let it ring out, and then she listened to her voice messages.

'Pippa?' He sounded puzzled. 'Where are you? Has something happened?'

His second message was more anxious.

'Are you all right, Pippa? Call me!'

The third was a mixture of worry and anger.

'Look, if I've said or done anything to upset you, I'm sorry. Call me.'

The text he'd sent just said: Where are you?

She sat on her sofa and took some deep breaths. There was no point in getting into a state about this. She had to be rational and cool-headed. She needed to get a grip on herself, but it was hard. She felt so hurt, and she felt as though her heart was broken.

She took another deep breath and picked up her phone. She dialled Gerry's number.

'Pippa! What on earth is going on?'

'I'm sorry,' she said as calmly as she could. 'Sudden family emergency. I had to rush.'

'You scared me,' he said. 'You should have left a message.'

82

'Sorry,' she repeated.

'Is there anything I can do?'

'Not at all. It's under control now.'

'Well . . . can you come back?'

'I'm afraid not.'

'Do you want to meet again?' He was sounding uncertain.

'I'm busy next week,' she said. 'Travelling.'

'Oh. Where?'

Hah! She thought. I knew it. He wants to know about my customers.

'Plymouth,' she said.

'Plymouth? There are people needing your computer skills in Plymouth?'

'And why shouldn't there be?' she demanded.

'No reason. No reason at all. It's just . . .' His voice trailed off. 'Will you be back at the weekend?'

'I hope so.'

'Well, look . . . can I call you?'

'Sure,' she said. She allowed her voice to soften because it had suddenly occurred to her that if he could play this game, she could too. 'I'm really sorry, Gerry. It was so sudden. I had to rush off.'

'Are you sure everything is all right?'

'Yes. It wasn't as bad as everyone thought. A bit of a storm in a teacup actually.'

'If you're sure . . .'

'Of course,' she said. 'Sorry if I was abrupt. I was all over the place.'

'That's OK.' He sounded relieved. 'I thought I'd done something to drive you away.'

'Not at all.' Pippa was proud of the way she was managing to get it all together again. 'Thank you for a wonderful day.'

'I had a great time,' said Gerry. 'I really did.'

'Me too.'

Neither of them spoke for a minute.

'So,' she said. 'I'd better go.' She paused, and then asked him casually where he was travelling to for the coming week.

'Oh, Glasgow,' he said. 'There's a new business park up there that I'm hoping will pay dividends.'

'Really?' she said. 'All those companies need a consultant like you?'

'Hopefully.'

'Have fun with it,' she told him.

'You too. Enjoy Plymouth.'

'I will.'

'And I'll call you.'

'Sure.'

'OK. So . . . good night, Pippa.'

'Good night, Gerry.'

'Sleep well.' His voice was soft.

'You too.'

She ended the conversation. The tears were rolling down her cheeks again. She sat down in the armchair. Hobo, who'd followed her into the flat when she'd come home, jumped on to her lap. Here we go again, she thought, as she stroked his head. Me and the cat all alone together.

Pippa woke up with a throbbing headache the following morning. Her eyes were puffy from crying and she felt terrible. But she was angry too. How dare Gerry Williams treat her like that? Who the hell did he think he was? She wasn't going to let him take advantage of her. She wasn't going to let him steal her clients and wreck her chance of a trip to New York. He'd messed with the wrong girl!

She opened her laptop and Googled business parks in Glasgow. The only one she could find that she hadn't been to before was called Earl's Seat Business Estate, about twenty miles outside the city. There were a variety of companies listed for the estate and she checked their websites carefully. If she was right about Earl's Seat, and Gerry Williams was targeting the same type of companies as her, there were three or four that might fit the bill.

She made a list so that when she went into the office the next day she could start calling them straightaway.

When she'd first come to work in sales, she'd hated phoning people she didn't know to make appointments. Richard had told her that cold-calling was an important part of the business, and that she'd have to get over it. She'd got better and better at it, but it was her least favourite part of her job.

The first three people she called on Monday said that they didn't need computer security. Pippa told them that everyone needed security, but she knew she was wasting her time. The fourth person was a cheerful girl with a friendly voice. Her name was Fiona and she told Pippa that she'd be happy to meet her. But, said Fiona, her company didn't have a lot of money to spend on swanky systems. Pippa said that she was sure they could work something out. She was relieved that Fiona hadn't mentioned anything about Safety Net. Nobody had, not even the companies who'd said they weren't interested in talking to her. Maybe, she thought, she'd made a mistake. Maybe she'd picked the wrong place.

Now that she had one possible customer, she wanted to make sure she got more. She rang everyone on her list and managed to get another two appointments. Then she called some of her old customers in the city. She told them she was visiting the area and she'd drop in. They were pleased to hear from her.

She decided it would be more efficient to fly to Glasgow and hire a car for her trip. She got an early flight from Heathrow the following day and arrived in Glasgow at 9.30. She picked up the keys to her Fiesta at the rental desk and then set out for her first meeting.

It was warm and humid, with a hint of thunder in the air. There were big purple clouds on the horizon. She was sure it would rain later. She hoped she'd get most of her calls done before it did. She didn't like rain.

It took her half an hour to find the business estate. It was out in the countryside, with wonderful views towards the wide river. The estate was new and the buildings were all low-rise. They were mostly steel and glass, reflecting the purple clouds, and they were set in a square around a big fountain. It would be a nice place to work, thought Pippa. There was a feeling of space and light that was always missing in London.

She checked which building she wanted for her first meeting, which was with the cheerful girl, Fiona. She pushed open the door and went inside.

The receptionist told her to wait for a few minutes. Pippa sat down in one of the leather chairs. She hoped that this wouldn't be like Luton. That she wouldn't see Gerry suddenly coming out of the office ahead of her!

Luckily Fiona was on her own. She greeted Pippa and brought her up to the second floor. She explained the system that they had. It was a small system and very simple. Pippa asked Fiona to log out. Then she sat down and hacked into it.

'Oh my God!' said Fiona. 'How did you do that?'

'It's all too easy,' said Pippa. 'But it wouldn't be possible if you used Defender. It's especially good if you bring your laptop home at night.'

'I do,' said Fiona. 'We all do. It's a small company.'

'I know,' said Pippa, 'and I know that you can't spend a fortune on security. That's why I have a special offer for you.'

She'd worked this out with Richard. To compete with Safety Net's twenty-four-hour phone service, they were doing a big discount for the first three months. It included round-the-clock phone assistance for that time.

'It's still a bit pricey.' Fiona sounded doubtful.

'But great value,' said Pippa.

Fifteen minutes later she left the office with a signed contract. She clenched her fist in triumph. Got you, Gerry Williams, she thought. Nobody tries to fool me. Nobody gets the better of me. And nobody steals my New York trip from under my very nose.

Chapter Ten

Pippa was on her final call in the Earl's Seat Business Estate when it happened. She walked into the reception area of the office. The receptionist told her that Jim Black, the man she was to meet, had been delayed. He'd been visiting one of the company's sites on the other side of Glasgow and had got caught up in traffic. He was running about twenty minutes late.

Pippa said that it didn't matter and that she'd wait. The receptionist printed a name badge for her. Pippa pinned it to her jacket and sat down on one of the chairs. She took a copy of the local paper from the glass-topped table. It was always worth reading local papers, she thought. They gave you things that you could talk about to the customers.

She was reading about the amateur dramatic society's successful performance of *My Fair Lady* when the door opened. She looked up, expecting that Jim Black had finally returned. But it wasn't the managing director who walked in. It was Gerry Williams.

He was wearing his suit again. His hair was gelled. He had his briefcase. He looked very confident. Pippa held her paper up in front of her face. Gerry hadn't seen her.

He walked over to the reception desk and said that he had an appointment with Jim Black. The receptionist told him about the traffic delay, and also told him that Mr Black had another person waiting to see him, so Gerry might be waiting for quite some time. She waved towards Pippa as she spoke, and Gerry looked over.

Pippa lowered the newspaper. Gerry's eyes opened wide in surprise.

'Pippa,' he said. 'What are you doing here?'

He pinned his name badge on to his lapel as he walked over to her.

'Why are you here?' he said again. 'I didn't know you were planning to be in Scotland this week. I thought you were in Plymouth.'

'Change of plans,' she said.

'So why are you meeting Jim Black?' he asked. 'Do you know him? Does the company buy your computers? Is that it?'

Pippa could feel herself blushing, but she was determined not to look embarrassed.

'No,' she said. 'I'm hoping to sell our product to him.'

'You sell computers!' Gerry was astonished. 'I thought you were a programmer.'

'You seemed to make that assumption,' she agreed.

'So . . . what *do* you do with computers then?'

'I sell software security programmes,' she told him.

His eyes narrowed.

'You're a salesperson?'

'Yes.'

'You sell security programmes?'

'That's what I said.'

'Who do you work for?' asked Gerry.

'Defender,' she told him.

His breath escaped slowly. 'Defender!'

'Yes,' she said. 'So why are you here, Gerry? Are you doing some consulting for Mr Black? Talking to him about strategy or something? About how to move his company forward?'

'No,' said Gerry.

'What then?'

'I'm a sales consultant,' he said.

'You mean a salesperson? Like me?'

'Yes,' said Gerry.

'Selling?'

'I think you already know.' Gerry frowned. 'You seem to have . . .' His expression was puzzled. 'How . . .'

'Oh, cut the crap,' she said. Her voice was suddenly sharp. 'You knew I worked for Defender. You probably worked it out when you first saw me in Birmingham. You knew where all my best customers were and that's why you were following me around England!'

'Are you bonkers?' demanded Gerry. 'You're talking complete nonsense. Of course I didn't know who you were. I thought we agreed that you were following me . . . oh!' He gasped. 'You were. You only came out with me to find out more about my customers. It was all a scam. You wormed your way into my flat and you came up with an excuse to get me out of the house just so's you could snoop . . .'

'Now who's being bonkers?' cried Pippa. 'How could I possibly have known that you didn't have water in your fridge? I said I'd drink tap water, for heaven's sake. I didn't get you out of the house.'

'You would have come up with something else,' retorted Gerry. 'I've heard all about you.'

'Oh, really?'

'Yes,' he said. 'Everywhere I go they talk about the great sales team at Defender – especially the girl. The best sales person in the country, they said. A really smart operator. They just called you Miss Jones and of course I never realised . . . never thought . . . how could I guess that you'd try to pull a fast one on me?'

'I did not!' she hissed.

'Was it you who told Tessa Bond that Safety Net wasn't worth a button and that you could hack it in seconds?'

Pippa shrugged.

'And said that a child of five could rewrite our software?'

She said nothing.

'And then you cut your prices and copied our phone helpline.'

'Well who on earth came up with that crazy twenty-four-hour phone assistance?' she cried. 'For heaven's sake, people are stupid enough already when it comes to their computers. You want to hold their hands twenty-four hours a day! So we had to make an offer.'

'And you're here now to do a pitch?' He stared at her.

'Yes.'

'Even though you told me you were going to Plymouth.'

'Yes.'

He was still staring at her. Then he slapped his leg with his hand in anger.

'You came here because I said I was coming

here!' he cried. 'You're trying to get to my clients first.'

'No,' she said. 'I talked it over with my boss and we felt that there were opportunities in Glasgow . . .'

'I don't believe it!' Gerry shook his head. 'All the time I really liked you, but you were stringing me along.'

'No I wasn't,' she said. 'You were stringing me.'

As they glared angrily at each other, Jim Black came into the reception area. He looked at both of them.

'Miss Jones,' he said. 'Mr Williams. I'm sorry you two have bumped into each other. I don't normally have that happen. I'm also sorry I'm late, and that I can't see either of you right now.'

'It's nice to finally meet you,' said Pippa. She held out her hand and Jim Black shook it.

'We've had a crisis on one of our sites,' he said. 'I'm going to have to go out again. I'm really sorry. We'll have to make it another day.'

'Are you sure you don't have fifteen minutes?' said Gerry. 'Because I can run through—'

'I'm sorry,' said Jim Black again. 'I have to leave. If you ring again tomorrow, I'll try to fit you in. Now if you'll excuse me, I need to get some things from my office before I go out.'

He walked towards the stairs. Pippa moved as though to follow him. Gerry grabbed her by the arm.

'Let go of me,' she said.

'You're not going after that man,' said Gerry.

She shook his hand from her arm. 'I wasn't,' she lied.

She unpinned her badge and handed it back to the receptionist.

'Can you arrange a meeting for tomorrow?' she asked.

'Of course,' said the receptionist.

'As early as possible,' said Pippa.

As the receptionist looked at the diary in front of her, Pippa saw Gerry walking out of the building. She watched him getting into a red car. Where was he going? What was his next call? Wherever it was, she wanted to be there first.

'Nine o'clock?' said the receptionist.

'That's fine,' said Pippa. 'Thanks. Got to rush.'

She hurried out to the car park and got into the Fiesta. Gerry was just turning on to the main road. She started the car and followed him. It seemed to Pippa that they were going further into the country. There were fewer and fewer buildings around. Then she realised where he was headed. It was a manufacturing plant about ten miles away, a company that relied a lot on IT. It was on her list of possible customers. She'd tried to get an appointment with the IT manager there before, but he had always refused to see her. She'd tried again for this trip too but still had no luck. Had Gerry? She gritted her teeth. There was no way he was going to get a meeting when she couldn't!

He turned up the side road that led to the factory. Pippa followed him. He was stopped at the security barrier. He spoke to the security guard and the barrier was lifted. It came down again in front of Pippa's car.

'I'm with him,' she told the security guard.

'Miss Pippa Jones?'

'Yes.' She looked surprised.

'I'm sorry, madam,' said the security guard. 'The gentleman said that you were no longer with Safety Net.'

'What?'

'He said that you'd been fired.'

'What?'

'He said that you were unreliable.'

'Oh!' Pippa's cheeks were red with fury. As she sat in her car behind the barrier, she saw Gerry get out of his. He turned towards the barrier, and waved at her.

She banged her hand on the steering wheel in annoyance as she watched Gerry enter the building. Then the purple clouds finally decided to chuck down the rain. Big fat drops splattered the windscreen of the car. The windscreen wipers moved faster to cope with them as she turned the car around and drove back towards the city.

It was a couple of hours until her next meeting, so she stopped off in a café and ordered a coffee and a sandwich.

She was still angry: angry with Gerry; angry with herself; angry with everything. How dare he think that she'd gone out with him just to get information? She'd gone out with him because she liked him, and cared about him! She'd never met anyone like him before. She'd never felt as close to another person before. They liked the same things. They seemed to connect. Well, they had seemed to connect. Not now, of course.

She stared out of the café window as the rain pelted against it. He was so wrong about her. But, she thought unhappily, maybe she'd been wrong about him too. She'd thought the same things about him as he'd thought about her. And she really had followed him to Glasgow! He had a right to be mad at her. She'd let her ambition get in the way of her feelings. She'd let a weekend in New York matter to her more than a wonderful day in London.

She'd been an idiot, and behaved like one too.

The rain had eased off a little. Pippa finished her coffee and sandwich and then drove to her next meeting. She was half expecting to see Gerry's car already parked outside the office. But there was no sign of it.

She went in and met with the IT manager. He was a chatty man, who was impressed by Defender. She explained all of the advanced security features. He nodded. 'We have some of those with our current system,' he said. 'But now that everyone in the office has laptops, we want to be more secure. It's so easy to leave one behind somewhere. Well, you read about it all the time, don't you? If MI5 can lose a laptop, what hope is there for the rest of us?' He smiled cheerfully at her.

'Exactly,' she said, 'but at least with Defender you can be certain that your information is secure.'

'Well, I'm convinced.' He held out his hand and shook hers. 'I'll get the contracts signed and send them to you next week.'

'Thank you,' she said.

'We were looking at another system,' he said. 'Safety Net, but it's a bit too basic for us.'

'It's a good system,' she said. 'Just not quite as advanced.'

He smiled. 'Not often you hear competitors praising each other.'

'Not often we do,' she said. 'I appreciate the business. Thank you.'

'We'll be in touch.'

Pippa walked out of the office and got into her car. That had been her last call. Overall the day had been very successful. Two definite contracts, other possibilities, and there was still Jim Black to see the next day.

She drove back to her hotel and checked in. She went to her room and lay on the bed.

Yes, it had been a good day.

It was a pity that she felt so miserable at the end of it.

Chapter Eleven

Pippa arrived at Jim Black's office at five to nine the next morning. This time the manager was ready to see her. She made her presentation and he said that it was very interesting. He told her that he'd get back to her. He said that he was considering a number of different systems.

'That's fine,' she said. 'Whatever works best for you.'

He raised his eyebrows slightly. 'I thought you'd tell me not to even consider anything else.'

She shrugged. 'I think we're the best, but it's what you think that's important.'

'Interesting way of looking at it,' he said.

She left the building. She didn't know if she'd get the deal or not. Even if she did . . . well, she wasn't sure it had been worth staying an extra day in Scotland for. Originally she hadn't intended to stay overnight, but when the meeting had been changed, she didn't have a choice.

She sighed. She felt miserable again. She was annoyed with herself for feeling like this.

Despite everything, she couldn't be absolutely certain that Gerry Williams hadn't been following her before, could she? Sales was a cut-throat business, after all. She gripped the steering wheel a little tighter. She wasn't sure about anything any more. Yet she couldn't help thinking that as far as Gerry was concerned she might have made a terrible mistake.

She dropped the car back with the rental agency and went into the airport. She checked in for her flight back to London and walked to the gate. There were already a lot of people waiting for the flight to be called, and she sat down between a tall man and a short woman. The man was tapping away at his mobile phone. The woman was reading a gossip magazine. Pippa read little bits of it over her shoulder. The same celebrity who'd been on the new diet the previous week now had a new boyfriend too. If only real life was as simple, thought Pippa.

Gerry Williams arrived just before they started to board. He saw her straightaway but didn't acknowledge her. Oh hell, she thought, I've messed things up really badly.

Her seat was at the front of the plane but Gerry's was further back. If they'd been sitting beside each other she would have talked to him. In fact, she would have apologised to him because she was beginning to realise that he hadn't made a fool of her. She'd made a fool of herself. She would have liked to tell him that and to explain how important Salesperson of the Year and the trip to New York was. She would have liked to say that she wasn't usually so stupid. But there was no chance of speaking to him now.

I wish I could stop thinking about him, she thought as the plane lifted into the sky. I wish he didn't matter to me!

They arrived at Heathrow five minutes early. Pippa took her bag from the overhead bin and got off the plane. She was halfway to the arrivals area when Gerry caught up with her.

'I hope you had a successful meeting this morning,' he said.

She felt her heart beat a little faster. At least he was speaking to her again.

'I hope so too,' she replied, 'and I hope you had a successful meeting yesterday.'

'Yes, I did,' he told her. 'Thanks for making sure I got there safely.'

She glanced at him.

'Honestly!' His voice was suddenly amused. 'Following me! To Glasgow. To my meetings. You're obsessed, Pippa Jones. You know that, don't you?'

'I might have lost it a little bit,' she said.

'A lot,' he told her.

'Look, I'm sorry . . .'

'It doesn't matter.' He was dismissive. 'It's in the past.'

He continued to stride through the airport and she walked beside him. The doors to the arrivals area opened and he smiled suddenly. A woman who was waiting outside waved at him. She was tall and thin. Her hair was caramel and honey. She was wearing a green dress that clung to her perfect figure.

'Amy!' he cried. He hurried over to her. She put her arms around him.

Pippa looked at them for a moment. She felt a lump in her throat. Damn it, she thought. I got it wrong again! I was starting to think that maybe things were all right between us, but he thinks I'm a complete flake. No wonder he's moving on to someone else! She turned away from him and Amy and walked quickly towards the trains. She was going to devote herself to her work from now on. She wasn't going to think about men. Not as lovers. Not as competitors. Not at all.

It would make life so much easier.

Things were better the following day. At least as far as work was concerned. Jim Black's company rang to say that they were interested in Defender. Another customer asked for some upgraded services. One of the people she'd visited in Birmingham phoned to say that he was sending a signed contract.

Richard called her into his office and told her that she was well on the way to beating her own record. That she was ahead of the sales she'd made this time last year.

She smiled at him and said that she was pleased about that. Richard looked curiously at her and told her that he'd thought she'd be over the moon. She insisted that she was. She said that she couldn't wait to go to New York, all expenses paid.

She stayed late in the office and then walked slowly home. The sun was still shining but she felt cold inside. She went up the steps to her flat and let herself in. She changed out of her suit into a T-shirt and one of her denim skirts. Hobo mewed at the door and she let him in. She opened a tin of tuna and put some in a saucer for him.

Then she picked up her phone and called Sherry. There was no answer. Pippa left a message on her voice mail asking her to call her. She rang Lissa too, but she didn't pick up either. This time Pippa didn't bother to leave a message.

A tear trickled slowly down her cheek. She was a hopeless case, she told herself. Her friends were too busy to talk to her. The man she'd fallen for had found someone else. She couldn't even enjoy the fact that her career was going well, because she was too miserable about Gerry to care.

She sighed. She'd never been too miserable to care before, even when Mark had split up with her. It had been totally different then.

She took her sketchbook out to the garden with her and began to draw. This time the picture was of Gerry standing next to the London Eye. Before she'd messed it all up, before she'd behaved like an idiot. It was a happy, sunny picture that didn't match her mood.

Hobo walked over to her and jumped up on to her lap. She put the drawing book on the garden table in front of her. Back to the future, she said to herself. Back to being comforted by a cat!

The doorbell buzzed. Maybe it was Lissa, she thought hopefully. Perhaps she'd seen her missed call and had been nearby and decided to drop in. Lissa was good in a boyfriend crisis. She'd been great after Mark, really supportive. Pippa felt that she needed support right now. She was tired of trying to do it all by herself.

She opened the door.

It wasn't Lissa.

It was Gerry.

He was leaning against the wall. He was wearing jeans and a T-shirt, and his hair was mussed.

'Oh,' she said. 'Hello.'

'Hi.'

'How did you know where I lived?' she asked.

He smiled. 'It wasn't hard to track you down. Not when I knew where you worked.'

'You followed me!' She looked at him with a mixture of anger and concern.

'You followed me before,' he reminded her. 'I just took a leaf out of your book.'

'I'm sorry about that,' she said. 'I was out of order.'

'Yes, you were.'

'I didn't mean . . .'

'Look, can I come in?' asked Gerry. 'Or are we going to have this discussion on the doorstep?'

She opened the door wider and led the way to the garden.

'Nice,' he said as he sat on one of the garden chairs.

'Thanks.' She suddenly remembered that the drawing book with his picture was on the table. She hoped he wouldn't notice it.

'So,' he said. 'You were apologising to me.'

'I've done with that,' said Pippa. 'I was wrong to follow you and wrong to try to steal your customers.'

'Thank you,' said Gerry.

'But you were wrong to get to know me and pretend that you cared about me.'

'What makes you think I was pretending?' he asked.

She shrugged. 'The girl waiting for you at the airport, for one thing.'

'Amy,' he said.

'Yes. Amy.' Who was easily as beautiful as a celebrity, who clearly cared about him, and who wasn't mad as a hatter either!

'She's my half-sister,' said Gerry, 'from my dad's second marriage.'

'Oh!' Pippa looked embarrassed. 'Well, she gave you a very big hug.'

Gerry laughed. 'I hadn't seen her in ages, and she's an affectionate girl.'

'OK, OK, I keep getting things wrong!' cried Pippa. 'The thing is – I thought you'd figured out my job. When I was alone in your flat, I went through the papers for something to read, and I saw the Safety Net brochure. You said you were a consultant. I didn't think you meant sales consultant. But when I saw the brochure, the penny dropped.'

This time Gerry looked a little embarrassed. 'To be honest, I was trying to sound important,' he confessed. 'When we met in the hotel, you were so confident and so pretty and I liked you straightaway. When you said you worked in computers I thought if I admitted to being a sales rep you'd think I wasn't worth your while.'

'Gerry!' She was horrified. 'What a crazy thing to think! I'm a sales rep, for heaven's sake. I don't care what anyone does for a living.'

'I didn't know that then,' he said. 'It was just ... I wanted to get to know you, but I didn't think you'd be bothered with me.'

A sudden gust of wind blew the pages of her drawing book. As Gerry reached out to stop them scattering around the garden, he saw the drawing of himself.

'What on earth . . . ?' He frowned. 'Who gave this to you?'

'Nobody,' she said. 'I did it myself.'

He looked at it without speaking.

'A hobby,' she told him. 'It relaxes me.'

He smiled. 'I'm glad you thought I was a good subject.'

She smiled too. 'You were on my mind,' she admitted.

'Really?'

'Yes.'

'So . . . you think there might be something between us?' he asked. 'Enough to keep me on your mind?'

'I . . .'

'From the first moment I met you, in Birmingham, I felt a connection,' said Gerry quickly.

'Maybe it's just the connection of us both being in sales,' she said.

'No, a different connection. And I was right,' he added. 'There's the country music . . .'

'And the adventure holidays . . .'

'And the chips.' His blue eyes twinkled.

'Those too,' she agreed.

'And there was something else as well.'

She looked at him. Her expression was puzzled.

'This.'

He moved towards her and put his arms around her. Then he kissed her.

There was something very right about being kissed by Gerry Williams. Something to do with the softness of his mouth and the strength of his arms around her. Something to do with the spicy scent of his aftershave and the feel of his cheek against hers.

She kissed him too. She wasn't thinking about sales numbers or customers, or weekends in New

York. She wasn't thinking of anything at all other than that this was a perfect moment in her life.

He broke away from her, but he still kept his arms wrapped around her.

'So,' he said.

'So what?'

'So is there a truce in the Security Wars?'

She grinned.

'Maybe.'

'Are we agreed that we both have the same job, and that neither of us is following the other person?'

She nodded.

'Are we agreed that we're not spying on each other?'

She nodded again.

'And are we agreed that you're coming out to dinner with me tonight?'

She smiled. Then she nodded once more.

'Excellent,' said Gerry. 'I know a place that does great chips.'

Then he tightened his hold on her and kissed her again, which meant neither of them needed to say anything at all.

Quick Reads 📖

Books in the Quick Reads series

Quick Reads 📖

Great stories, great writers, great entertainment

Quick Reads are brilliantly written short new books by bestselling authors and celebrities. Whether you're an avid reader who wants a quick fix or haven't picked up a book since school, sit back, relax and let Quick Reads inspire you.

We would like to thank all our partners in the Quick Reads project for their help and support:

Arts Council England
The Department for Business, Innovation and Skills
NIACE
unionlearn
National Book Tokens
The Reading Agency
National Literacy Trust
Welsh Books Council
Basic Skills Cymru, Welsh Assembly Government
The Big Plus Scotland
DELNI
NALA

Quick Reads would also like to thank the Department for Business, Innovation and Skills; Arts Council England and World Book Day for their sponsorship and NIACE for their outreach work.

Quick Reads is a World Book Day initiative.
www.quickreads.org.uk   www.worldbookday.com

Quick Reads 📖

Great stories, great writers, great entertainment

Men at Work

Mike Gayle

Hodder

A sweet, funny story about love and work

Ian Greening loves his job. He loves it so much he won't even take a promotion. He'd rather muck about with his workmates.

The other love of his life is girlfriend Emma. They've been together for years. The problems start when Emma loses her job and gets a new one in Ian's office. Ian doesn't like it at all. No more mucking about. No more flirting with the girls in admin. Ian wants her out. The question is, how? Can he do it without losing her or will it all end in tears?

Quick Reads 📖

Great stories, great writers, great entertainment

Strangers on the 16:02

Priya Basil

Black Swan

A very ordinary train journey goes horribly wrong

It's a hot, crowded train. Helen Summer is on her way to see her sister Jill and tell her an awful secret. Another passenger, Kerm, is on his way back from his grandfather's funeral. They are strangers, jammed against each other in a crowded carriage. Noisy school kids fill the train – and three of them are about to cause a whole heap of trouble. In the chaos, Helen and Kerm are thrown together in a way they never expected. Catching a train? Read *Strangers on the 16:02* and you'll never feel the same way about your fellow passengers again.

Quick Reads 📖

Great stories, great writers, great entertainment

Clouded Vision

Linwood Barclay

Orion

A chilling story of double-dealing, violence and murder

Ellie wakes covered in blood. She's trapped in a car, on a frozen lake. CRACK. The ice is breaking. One more crack and the car will plunge into the water below, taking Ellie with it …

Meet Keisha Ceylon – she's a nasty piece of work. She tricks families with visions she says will lead them to missing loved ones. However, one of those dodgy visions gets too close to the truth. Someone doesn't like it – and they're ready to kill to keep a terrible secret safe.

This chilling tale from bestselling writer Linwood Barclay will make your blood run cold.

Quick Reads 📖

Great stories, great writers, great entertainment

Jack and Jill

Lucy Cavendish

Penguin

The disturbing tale of a young boy
and his devoted sister

Jill loves her little brother, Jack. She understands what he's thinking, which is just as well because Jack won't speak.

There are plenty of things Jill doesn't understand though. Why is her mum dumping her and Jack in the country? Why did her dad leave and she's not allowed to talk about it? She doesn't know why her aunt and uncle give her and Jack strange looks, or why they're being talked about in the village.

With a local country boy Jill decides to find out what's going on and uncovers the appalling truth behind brother Jack's silence.

Quick Reads

Great stories, great writers, great entertainment

Trouble on the Heath

Terry Jones

Accent Press

A comedy of Russian gangsters, town planners
and a dog called Dennis

Martin Thomas is not happy. The view he loves is about
to be blocked by an ugly building. He decides to take
action and organises a protest. Then things go badly
wrong and Martin finds himself running for his life. Along
the way he gets mixed up with depressed town
planners, violent gangsters and a kidnapped concert
pianist. Martin starts to wonder if objecting to the
building was such a good idea when he finds himself
upside down with a gun in his mouth.

This hilarious story from Monty Python star, Terry Jones,
will make you laugh out loud.

Other resources

Enjoy this book? Find out about all the others from
www.quickreads.org.uk

Free courses are available for anyone who wants to
develop their skills. You can attend the courses in your
local area. If you'd like to find out more, phone
0800 66 0800.

Don't get by get on 0800 66 0800

For more information on developing your basic skills in
Scotland, call The Big Plus free on 0808 100 1080 or visit
www.thebigplus.com

Join the Reading Agency's Six Book Challenge at
www.sixbookchallenge.org.uk

Publishers Barrington Stoke (www.barringtonstoke.co.uk)
and New Island (www.newisland.ie) also provide books
for new readers.

The BBC runs an adult basic skills campaign.
See www.bbc.co.uk/raw.

www.worldbookday.com